THE ADVENTURES OF BIC CALAMUS

THE ADVENTURES OF BIC CALAMUS

BY BIC CALAMUS

AuthorHouse™
1663 Liberty Drive
Bloomington, IN 47403
www.authorhouse.com
Phone: 1-800-839-8640

Published by AuthorHouse 08/21/2012

ISBN: 978-1-4772-2670-4 (sc)

To Adele..and Look!...
I know it's an Italian tradition in your family to rub watermelon in my face but please STOP!!
It's giving me the pip!!!
B.C

KOREAN FOR KIDS
Writers Block and You. what to?
Bhagavad Gita for babies

ADVISE RICHARD OBRIAN
ITS JUST BUREACRACY
BEING CRAZY AND TO HANG
IN THERE, RAHTER THAN
YOURSELF.

CONTACT BILL BENDER
AND SUGGEST USING
SERIAL MUSIC IF HE
WANTS TO BE TAKEN
SERIOUSLY

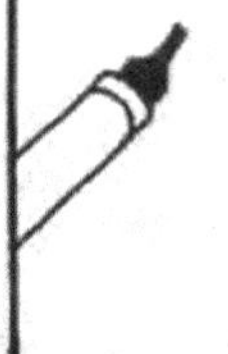

IN HOT PURSUIT OF THE PINK PANTHER: WHEN FACT AND CARTOON CHARACTERS COLLIDE
In a series of jewellery heists the criminal sensations who go by the name "Pink Panther Gang" are proving crime really does pay. With a penchant for pink panther suits the world is indeed their oyster, their most recent racket involving making off with the worlds most expensive pearl necklace.
LEARN THE PINK PANTHER ON THE PIANO... REMEMBER TWO PAWS...
RING RING
Mmmyello Bic speaking
?!?!
Ah...mmyello?
?!&#@!
Arh... Hello! This is 987654321...007.. WOULD YOU LIKE HELP ON YOUR HEARING AID WITH THAT?!

REEEEORW!!
I think therefore I ran...hmm... thats quite good
CLIK
Hey sorry Tabby...what's up?
Everything....
Ok...I'll check in with you later...
You should think about checking yourself in....
Hello Bic-Calamus and associates how may I help...
Oh hi dad...you want to talk to me?...yeah well I want to talk to you. is that going to work?
RING
RING

THIS IS NOT SMALL TALK
Yeah I said "Is that going to work?" not "Are you going to work?"
!?#@&!!
My hearing is fine..oh thats what you said..
Yes...ARE YOU GOING TO WORK IS WHAT I SAID..NOW WHAT HAVE YOU GOT TO SAY??
Well...I'm pleased you asked... I'm actually a writer now Dad.. call me Bic..
Yeah well write on... what are you writing about?!
A book on my year spent teaching English in Korea...It's to be called "Incomplete me-
Well I don't care what it's called ..I call it crazy
Well, it's full title is: "Incomplete Memoirs of a Complete Breakdown" and I've actually put a lot of effort into it...
Ah..F it son..you had better start making more sense... you owe me money!
You'll get your money pops...

Anyway read any good books lately?
What's going on there...apart from you and the floor...you still getting over yourself?
Rise and fall of the Roman Empire
G.Jibbons
Sorry..you were saying..
...I've just finished Ellisons Invisible man
Oh...and how did you find it??
If you really want to know...I found it almost impossible to pick up!
Yeah...I don't know what people see in that book...I must get around to reading it sometime... Anyway pops...gotta bounce. . .I have a radio interview. . .I'll get around to getting your money after I've spoken nicely to the landlord about possibly getting an extension
Seriously pops. . .if you saw me today you'd pick me as a pauper. . .
Yeah you always were a little fruity
U-C-lees
Dublins Pubs A conducted tour
ZEN and the art of FIXING your TRIKE
CLIK!

Oh man!
Late again!
BUS STOP
HEY WAIT!
SWANSTON
LIBRA
CITY
ARGH!

Er, sorry mate...
FLINDERS
PANT
PANT
PANT
PANT
ABC RADIO
oh

Hello and welcome ..you're with Bec and you and I are listening to ABC's 123.. With us in the studio we have a gentleman Bic-Calamus..who is here to discuss his latest novel 'Incomplete Memoirs of a Complete Breakdown'...Welcome Bic
ON AIR
Hi there..
Now Bic...that' a catchy title...want to tell us more?..
Yeah...well its essentially a series of essays written while living in Korea...I was there for a year teaching English and I assure you it wasn't plain sailing...
Go on..
Well have you ever tried using a toilet flush with the floor??
...What...You mean..
Yes...It was challenging to put it mildy....and to use them correctly you had to perform what people in the know know to be a 'kimchi squat"...
...what the hell is kimchi??
Oh just some kind of cabbage they leave to ferment for up to a year...
Sounds delicious...I actually prefer soggy cardboard

HAW HAW
HAW
HAW
HAW
HAW
Yeah just thinking about it unsettles me...
The kimchi??
No the toilet!
So tell us Bic...what's your real name...
...Er...It's personal
Ok..i get that...so where does Bic-Calamus come from
...well if you must know Bic-calamus is a type of pen name
Fascinating...Tell us more
HEY! NOW!
Well...I'm hoping it's something my readers pick up on...essentially it's a pen name in a very literal sense...
Bic is a cheap biro..one that breaks when you first pick it up...sometimes sooner...
...Some kind of ball-point pen huh?
..Yeah.. Write on...Well it is when it is working...
..and Calamus?
Thats part of my latin heritage.it also happens to be a slang word the Inuit Eskimos use meaning 'cold commode'...

..You wouldn't want to be in that continent..
And tell us Bic when did you first get an inkling you were a writer?
Umm..
Ahhh..
I guess it happened at college on getting an essay back...
From memory it was on Shakespeare...one of his lesser known tradegies..
Oh...which one Bic?
...er...arh...much ado about...er...something
..ar...Don't know if I have heard of this one
..No...Most people haven't...
..Anyway...about the essay ..what happened??
As it turned out...my teacher...using only what can be described as an illegible scrawl informed me that my essay was indeed well written and I had much potential as a writer...
...thats encouraging..
umm...I didn't take too much notice at the time...I still don't...it wasn't my essay he was marking..

Ehehehe...we may have to edit that Bic...we don't want our listeners thinking of you as a little out to sea...

..whatever floats your boat...

Now Bic...did you have any problems writing 'Incomplete Memoirs..'
yes ..I had many...essentially writing 'Incomplete' was one big problem..or rather problem solving exercise...the main problem being the rent...the landlord and how to avoid him altogether...
..I see...I hope he isn't listening...and writers block...you've never had a problem with that..

I GET UP!!.... AND NOTHIN GETS ME DOOOWN
yo..Van Halen and associates...what's up?

It's..it's my landlord...
what do I say??
Well just say hi like most
people do
Hello..you've reached the voice mail
box of Bic-calamus...please record
your beep after the tone
so what was that all about?
Oh just some imbroglio
with the land lord
Sounds like that's
something you really
should address.
Yeah well I haven't really
got an address...my
stuffs there but I'm
not...I cant really afford
to see the guy.
Anyway what was that
you were saying about
writers block??
I never get it
..what never??
No...I've actually developed
a cure for it...

Really...
yes I have...when you have it ...dont write...dont even attempt it...
um...
sounds logical..
if nothing else..

are..are you alright??
I..I.. just get so pensive
SNAP!
SOB
SOB
SOB
SOB
SOB
HEY NOW
Well Mr Calculus we all have our problems...

It's actually Calamus..
PFFF
It pays to differentiate between the two..
I guess I should lighten up
ON AIR
er..this is no smoking Bic..
TSSSS
The most difficult thing, but an essential one...is to love life..to love it even while one suffers, because life is all...life is God..and to love life means to love God..

That's an interesting quote...yours??

no ..Toy Story

Anyway....I hear the
local vodka is a little
hard to stomach..

.oh...you mean So-Ju...yeah it's like a mild form of
suicide...they prefer slamming it..taking hits until they
start missing their face altogether...

..I think I feel a
head ache coming on...

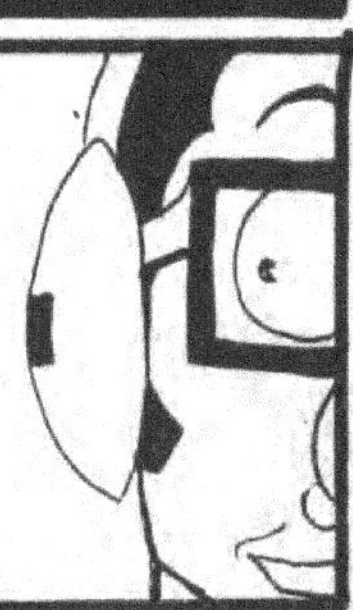
..yeah it has the uncanny
ability to begin and end
proceedings pretty much
straight away.

ok Bic ..unfortunately we have run
out of time...thanks for coming ..

you're welcome...
..and good luck with the next one...
ON AIR
HEY NOW
...cheers..
Seeya

RADIO
yeah well I'd misplaced my phone and had been perpending its whereabouts for some time...the bottom line was I'd been sitting on it!!
...hello ..prank caller...line poo..
TRAM STOP
7

...yes well his bra business went bust...I mean where else was it going to go?
...and hows the 'only at cinemas' voiceover enunciated in that hoarse, husky voice that could pass as a cement mixer... I mean where else is it going to be...
...fancy a tipple?..

it's apodictic you dick !!"
VIRES ACQUIRIT EUNDO

why run?...the rain is everywhere..
this rain is everywhere...arrhhh...get out of my face...
INCOMING CALL:
I GET UP!!... AND NOTHIN GETS ME DOOOWN

oh hi Tinea...im pleased you called...now about this graphic novel...you're happy to do it?.
yes...I can, it sounds like an interesting project...making news items into cartoons is certainly new to me..
..well as a graphic artist I want you go go above and beyond the call of duty...you know ..like take things to the next level..
you sound excited...
UNMANNED MANHOLE
..excited?!!...I'm practically erumpent ...I mean this shit is trippy...

OFFIC

DR. FU MANCHU
(OXFORD)
M.A.D.D.AS
(YALE)
P.O.C.O.L.O.C.O
(HARDLY)
Dream analysis, Sexual abnormalities and all other psychosomatic psychological problems you would rather not talk about
thanks for fitting me in Dr Fu

its a fix I'm hoping you will fix..
so..Bic...how would describe your relationship with yourself?
er ..well...rather uncomfortable in places
care to elaborate...?

Well...my moods for one thing...they are all over the place...
I see
I'm not sure I really do..

At times I feel like a poorly assembled blot on the landscape whereas other times I feel like a mercender map that is going places....
Fascinating metaphor...care to tell us more
yeah thanks for asking,,,psychologically I have been carrying out my own investigations...
Sounds dangerous...er I mean fascinating

yeah examining my own thoughts I confess was a little off putting...a bit like my golf

Now thats something I don't want to see...
This guy really is a little out to sea

...yes...well...concerning my thought patterns... I couldn't really find a pattern... I guess I found it all pretty much incomprehensible... much like some of the T-shirts in Korea...
does the name Bozo the Clown mean anything to you?
I'm...I'm...not sure I know what you mean
Well you're the Psychiatrist!! ...you should do...I pay you to...
...and lose the nervous stutter pal...
sure ...yeah I get that...just out of interest what foods do you like Bic?

well I enjoy flash fried duck...as opposed to sampling the soil in a vain attempt at trying to catch one...
er...this is no smoking Bic...
just out of interest how would you describe your schooling?
I wonder what the teachers thought of this character?
Bic Calamus
His psychological peregrinations have an undefined hazy quality marked by a direction best described as aimless and missing the point rather than any well defined X you would find on any reputable pirate map.
well the teachers didn't think that much of me..
Perhaps because you didn't think that much yourself...
Do you suppose that is because you didn't really apply yourself
why does this guy need to phrase things so formally??..he just needs to relax man..
well..I guess I just didn't give a continental

I would prefer if we kept a modicum of decorum..
Can you elaborate?
...and perhaps stretch your pea sized brain into something a little less vegetative than a neglected compost heap
well I'd like to blame the teachers but I believe the problem went a lot deeper than that...
...er...you're starting to lose me Bic...want to be a little less cryptic?
...sigh..the town itself was something of a backwater and didn't have much going for it...the chess sets sold came with the instruction 'FOR TWO PLAYERS' displayed boldly enough on the box to ensure you knew what you were getting yourself into..
like not much to check out...as in a little stale, mate...if you'll ..erm..excuse the punnery...heheh
..yeah...you could say it was a bit like a one horse town where 'give way' signs do just that...after one too many intoxicated and somewhat misguided karate kicks and a few uneasy nights in the rather compromising position of 45 degrees... they eventually find rest in a prostrate position.
...usually to the delight of passing dogs who suddenly have more options ...
...well put...anyway enough about me ...how do you find the psychiatry profession Dr Fu?

I am SO down with having a break from this #$%^^
well I'm pleased you asked...
I'll tell you something about this when you are interviewing me...anyway Bec..oops I mean Bic...do you appreciate fine art?
entering the psychiatry profession is one way of going to pieces..meeting YOU is another...
.. er.. you mean like Mic-hell ang-e-loo?
well yes he does spring to mind
of course...that shit takes art to new heights...... the Cistern Chapel is quite something...
er..I think you mean the "Sistine Chapel"..and you don't really know much about it do you?
..no not really...no education was a wash out...
...there..there ...there must have been something you learnt
that I very much doubt..

since when did this guy develop a stutter?...
not wanting to bewilder him with my variety of truths but I wonder if i should tell him about passing time by passing wind?
well ...I guess school taught me how to fart really well..
excuse me?..farting??..you want to clear this up?
yes..it was actually a type of competition...and yes on occasion the room was cleared
sounds great...
I wonder if I still have any Gin left...
yes ..it took me some time but I eventually got mine to sound like a small but determined aircraft carrier having problems taking off
Sounds more like take me away...
Phobias: What to look out for
Sexuality, dreams and what to do when penis ivy takes root
Split personalities: Leaving them before its too late for goodbye

Can I ask you a question?

you just did..but yes..I wont charge

I see here you your occupation is teaching...whats the classroom like these days?

quite simply not simpatico...dreadful really
trying to teach year ten mathematics is beyond anyones comprehension and jumping through the nearest window has never looked so good
clearly a way forward
sounds a little like self contained psychosis

theres just no way I'm going to tell him about the time I forgot the fundamentals of circle geometry...arkward
yeah I actually teach science as well ...or at least attempt it..

..any better?..
it is if I can find material to engage the students..lately weve been looking at a womens right to sell off someone elses sperm..I've asked them to find cases to argue
wow cases?..thats a lot of sperm..like move over Moby Dick..
a hands on assignment huh ...sounds interesting
this guy needs me
I'm actually trying to get this writing thing off home base..when i can get my damn grammar right...
sounds like youve done your dash...
..well..I don't know how to use those either...
do you happen to have any of your writing with you?..
..funny you should mention it..I do..heres a little something I prepared earlier...

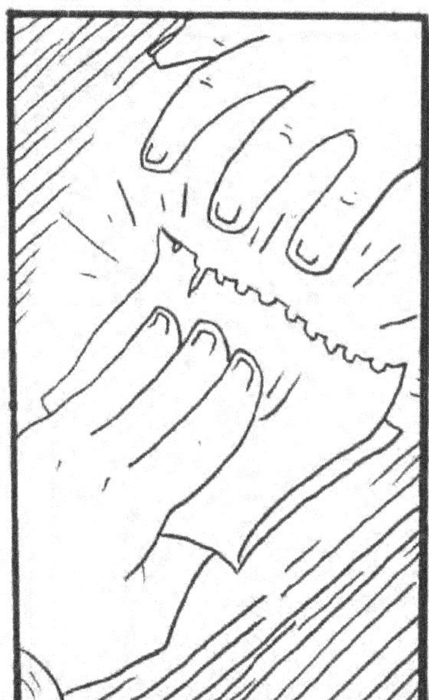

READING GLASSES STRONG ENOUGH TO PRODUCE VERTIGO AT A LEVEL SUGGESTING THE WORLD IS COMING OFF ITS AXIS

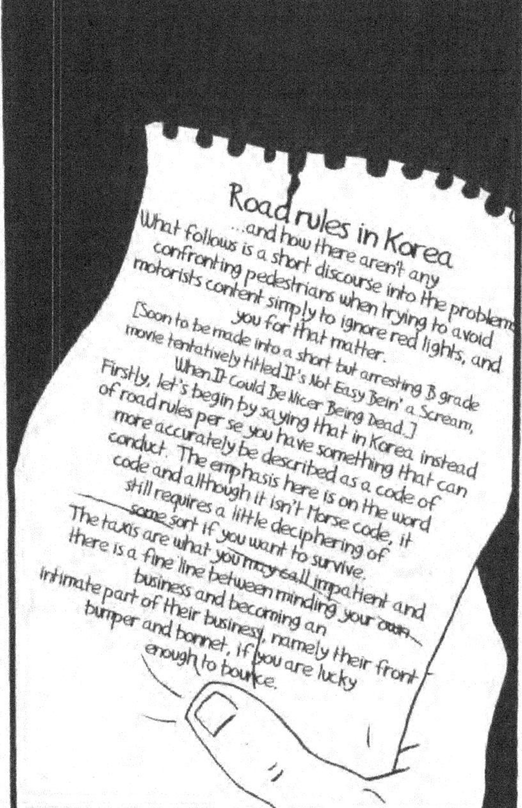
Road rules in Korea
...and how there aren't any
What follows is a short discourse into the problems confronting pedestrians when trying to avoid motorists content simply to ignore red lights, and you for that matter.
[Soon to be made into a short but arresting B grade movie tentatively titled It's Not Easy Bein' a Scream, When It Could Be Nicer Being Dead.]
Firstly, let's begin by saying that in Korea instead of road rules per se you have something that can more accurately be described as a code of conduct. The emphasis here is on the word code and although it isn't Morse code, it still requires a little deciphering of some sort if you want to survive.
The taxis are what you may call impatient and there is a fine line between minding your own business and becoming an intimate part of their business, namely their front bumper and bonnet, if you are lucky enough to bounce.

...so I take it getting from A to B was somewhat problematic
..yeah.. A and B were states..A stood for "Are you ok ??!" and B was "..Blood..group B...I...I...need the doc...."

oh...tempus fugit ...gotta fly Bec...

er.. its Bic...Bec is actually a girls name..
nothing is as it appears and behind that its all pretty much pear shaped...
..oh sorry Bic...I should get my head read...we'll see you next time.
CAT FOO
GENERIC BUSINESS OFFICES

yeah well...she was a little discontented...telling me I was a bit of a **let down**..that sort of thing

...like someone let me out I want to get off...so what did you do??

hey Dunkin ..its me Bic...how are you?

are you ok?...you sound drunk Dunkin.

well..I had to admit I needed a helping hand so I got hold of some Viagra..extra strength...

anyway I've come up with this great idea we can post on youtube...we are going to review all of Melbournes kool bars...sound cool?

...oh don't be silly...of course they'll let you in...

yes...you could say our relationship is now on the straight and narrow...
sorry...I mean people could be listening

so youre in...kool man...the camera man will be ready at nine sharp in the park...catch you..
CALL ENDED

SIMPLICITY FUNERALS
when you're carking there's no skylarking
relaxed funerals.. you dig?..
CAFE

7

SCHOOL
ATTENTION Please keep this gate closed at all times

its like...you know like...she knows he doesn't like her...
..yeah...like totally...I don't like him either...
ELEVATION HIGH: Endeavour to try
yeah like...um...like yeah...totally...
...ok...settle down year ten...I need your undivided attention...
today I've decided we are not in fact going to be doing algebra... but instead we are going to commence term two with a little circle geometry...
ALGEBRA 101: FOR DUMMIES

so get on with it... any problems let me know...

The great thing about teaching circle geometry is that any Bozo can do it..all you need is a large pair of blue shoes, an Elvis number ...and possibly a circus..

I...I don't know what's going on!
I'm not sure if i want to know what's going on

GULP!

I want a real teacher that knows what hes doing..

HA HA ..Mister Calculus doesn't know what he is doing!

er..its actually Calamus...now get back to work..

we'll come back to that one

when I can actually do it..oops

whatever..

WHITE
OUT

SPLOTCH

HAW HAW HAW HAHAHA HA HA HAW HAW

?!?
What the
@#$%^!!

sorry sir...
it was a mistake

BRRRIIIINGGGG
class dismissive
I mean dismissed.....
AND PHIL STINE YOU ARE COMING WITH ME!! TO THE PRINCIPAL!
sorry sir I cant...Im already expelled..I shouldn't really be here...have a good one
NO

Sometime later in the story
Feeling a little scrambled ??...your mind best described as 'mostly missing'..your memory following suit...or at least trying to..then you need ...
Dug Hollows Neurologist...specializing in most neurological neuroses and all manner of memory malfunction...
call 0800 123 123 007..thats 0800 123 132..oops I mean 123 007..over and not necessarily out...
Somewhere...be-yond the sea..somewhere waiting for me...my lover stands on golden sand and watches the ships that go sailing..
WHIRLED NEWS
Coming to a town named YOU!
TIGER WOODS: WOULD HE??!
Tiger Woods it seems makes achieving a low lying score both on and off the fairway look easy.
In the latest round of scandal surrounding the world's number one golfer it has been revealed he slept with over 120 girls. Winning the U.S masters seven times requires an iron will , as does juggling 120 mistresses. Fresh allegations suggest this is just a rough estimate and he is not out of the woods yet.
Pretty saucy huh?

SNAP!
Eventually the idea came to me...actually it whilst I was attempting sleep, not that I"d been doing much of it. Creditors all had my number and made no bones about letting me know they knew how to use it. I guess 98765432007 is a reasonably straight-forward number to remember.

to use it. I
straightforward
to remember.
Between fending off their calls and receiving unsolicited mail suggesting I should make a guest appearance in court the next day you could say things were rather unsettled.It was a case of not really knowing where to turn...feeling screwed if you like.
Anyway where was I ?..oh yes. The idea. It came to me whilst drifting off. Perched precariously somewhere halfway between the buoyant expectancy of a partially submerged submarine (yellow) and that inky uncertainty you find in any good horror movie where if anything is going to go bump it will. And rest assured a makeshift mumble of "It"s just me"...will not be forthcoming.
What people needed these days was a good divorce manual as everyone seemed to be doing it, with mixed results. With accusations being thrown around along with anything else that wasn"t tied down dissatisfied couples needed a more systematic approach to this apparent melange of mayhem
The title?
RING
RING
hi Bic...its Tinea ...just to let you know I have emailed you the graphic news article...
Oh thats great Tinea...thanks for that...
er...Im actually in a bit of a jam at the moment so if I can get those slides off you...would be good..
...sure.Tinea..I'll get your money....the machine ate my card the other day...so ill have to go to the bank...
(there wasn't a lot on it so hopefully it's not feeling too bilious)
..thanks Bic..
cheers..

Bic's Bank Esacape...

...or how to attract the wrong sort of interest

BANK OF TH

ENTRANCE

Bics financial predicament could be summed up by any word that sounds like something crash landing with plenty of Oomph!
Kaboom! would do it.
Visiting the bank was just part of it. This one act tragicomedy was a conjuring act involving as it did; a little fey enthusiasm on Bics part, a perplexed teller who until now had only used automated responses and a deferred audience that would rather be somewhere else...
329
463

Earlier that morning..
3:30 am..

In fact Bic was having problems sleeping and **yes** he was one big financial concern.

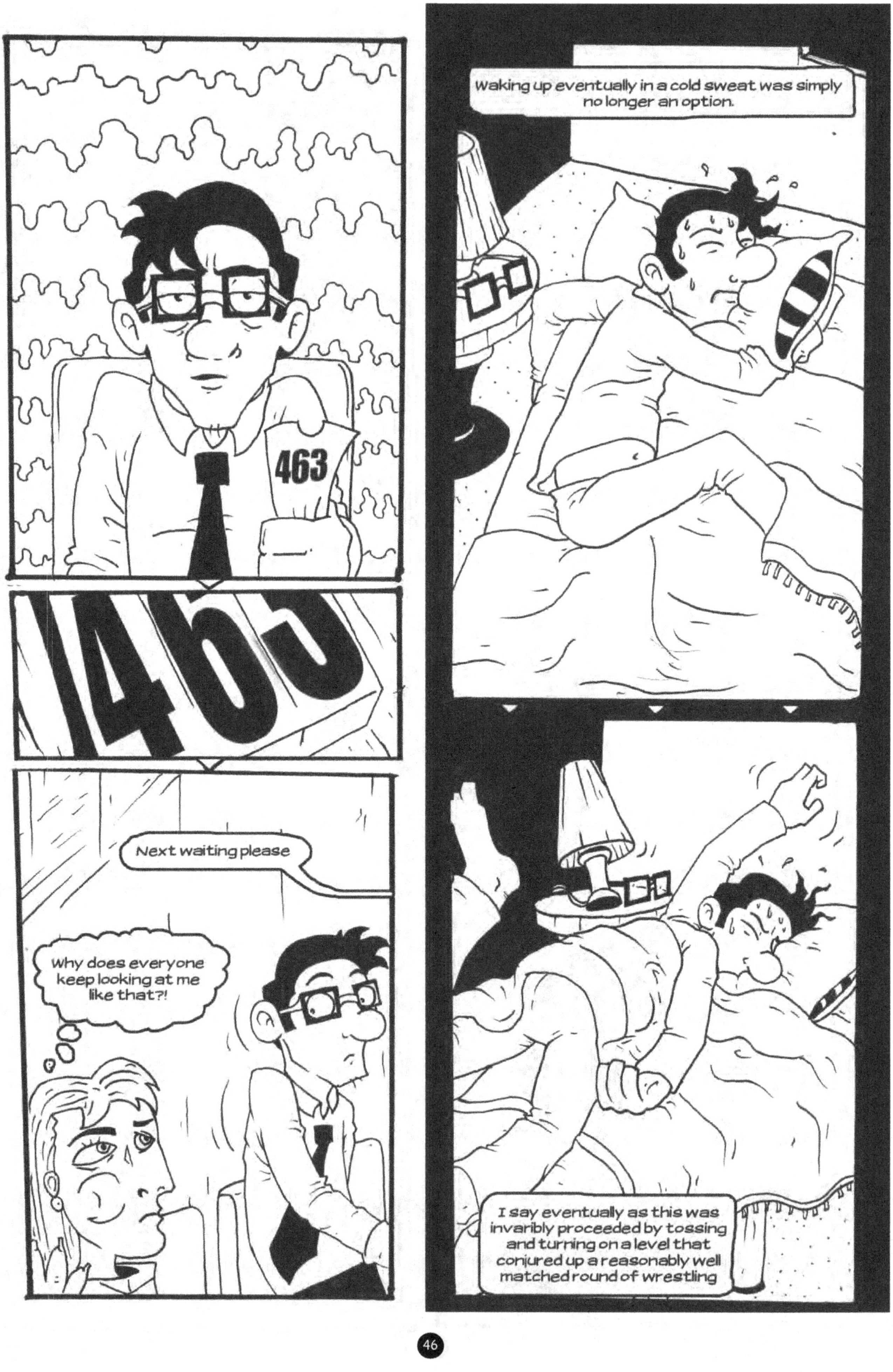

Waking up eventually in a cold sweat was simply no longer an option.

I say eventually as this was invaribly proceeded by tossing and turning on a level that conjured up a reasonably well matched round of wrestling

a withdrawal from this account if you will
Is this the money mum left me?
...the amount??

er...your'l need to be a little more specific Mr... ....Mr...Cal..cu..lus..
..yeah its actually Calamus ..
I can always count on someone getting that wrong..

It was a contortionists act even Houdini would be reluctant to get caught up in and shortly before waking up Bic would find himself on the floor somewhere.

A jumbled muddle of a puddle.

would that be
$2000
exactly..?

here goes nothing
yes

CLICK
CLICK

Account Status:
INACTIVE
Balance:
A large negative
number
Please see someone

It appears Mr..er Cal-a pus..

..its Cal-a-mus...whats
wrong with
you people??

WELL WHOEVER YOU ARE ..YOU.DON'T. HAVE.
ANY.MONEY. GET.IT ZIP.ZILCH.ZIPPO.JACK SQUAT.
..let me tell YOU something teller..
you...you.. you just rattle me....
...I demand to see the bank manager!

this guy is such a baby
you're just the icing on the cake you are!
have it your way....your bank doesn't interest me ANYWAY
I am the bank manager!
some days just feel like a dazed glaze...
I've heard of being overdrawn but that guy is ridiculous!
INCOMING CALL: Head Shrink
Hi Calamus and associated fallout...
hi Bic...It Dr Fu Manchu...look I've looked over your results and it appears you need a full psychometric psychoanalysis...
This guys timing is second to none...
are you sure?
quite sure...does two tuesday suit you..
..yeah...see you then...

GLUG
GLUG
GLUG

INTRODUCING:
Graphic Artist - Tin Wong

@: tin@thisyellowpencil.com
W: www.thisyellowpencil.com

Whirled News: Coming to a town named YOU!

IMPORTANT DISCLAIMER: The ideas presented here are NOT my own. If everything goes to plan (B...possibly C) I will be paid and be able to skip the country. T.W.

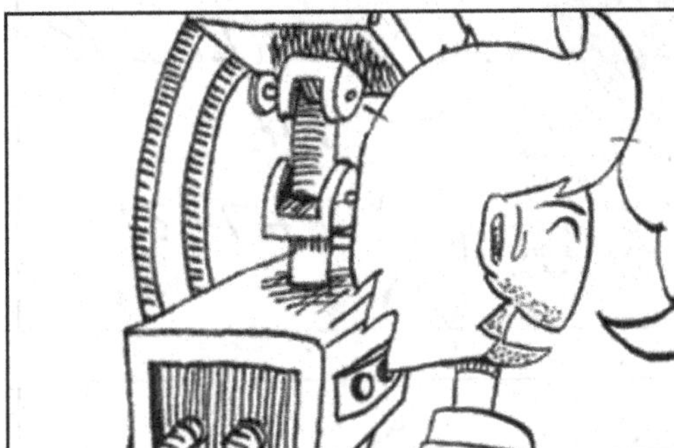

Get your butts ready people ... we're rolling in 60...seconds that is... don't blow it
Whirled News

well I don't f'in feel like fish tonite...you're just taking this healthy eating thing too far... stuff it.. I'm having Mackers

Make that forty...
...what...what do you mean...
Its got a sodium count of 3.2 grams for every..

THE FRUIT DOESNT HAVE A F'IN SODIUM COUNT
Not to mention a cholesterol count that does more than just add up

YOU AND YOUR BLOODY HEALTH FETISH... I WANT A TRIAL SEPARATION...

Hi God.. can you help me...

OMG..this guy really does need help...

Honey... you'll just end up bunching up in the wrong places

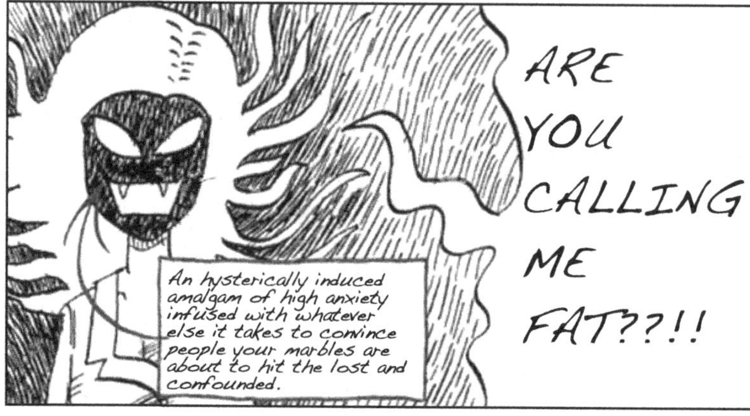
An hysterically induced amalgam of high anxiety infused with whatever else it takes to convince people your marbles are about to hit the lost and confounded.
ARE YOU CALLING ME FAT??!!

Of course not... just that you could be..we've been over this honey..
and rolling in ten

No actually they now have healthy options...even the O.J's taste fruit like...
dont buy into that nonsense sugar...it's like ...' do you want lies with that'

By the way...you're sleeping with her aren't you?...

Whirled News

PLOOP

Excuse me...

You heard me!

I'm sure most people did...
did you just let one rip?

You'll have to wrap this up people ... we're on air in ten
or at least what is left of it... you guys had better get your shit together...

ROLLING IN FIVE...
Uggh... thats enough to roll anyone PLACES PLEASE....

Uggh...you really need to put a stop to that
and... action..

Good morning folks and welcome to another edition of Whirled News: Coming to a town named you!
Well its been a pretty full week Teddy... the new Lady Goo-goo album seems to have broken a few records..but surely a more pressing issue is that of North Korea..just what are these guys up too

Your guess is as good as mine Barbie... the latest I hear is they are refusing to take any calls from anyone...

Yeah... U.S officials tried placing a call and ended up getting something that sounded offensive followed by a dial tone that was louder than it needed to be...

Yes.. turns out they contacted a Bull horn specialist that goes by the name Bill Bender to give it a go...

...well I've heard it all... a Bull horn specialist.. really??
Yes it seems if anyone could get their attention it was this guy.. he studied at the royal academy of music...apparently spent at least a year perfecting the C major scale at a volume suggesting somebody was on the verge of a mental breakdown...

Well that's news to me Teddy...
What do you mean Barbie...

I mean...nobody told me we were catching up with a fellow by the name of Bill Bender...
Well like Emerson said... life really is a series of surprises...and yes we are catching up with him... lets go to our European correspondent in Italy and see what he has to say...

Whirled News

Hello and welcome ..I'm Jack Binstalkin and with us in the open air we have Bill Bender a Bull horn specialist... welcome Bill..
Hi there...
Café Gatto Nero
Cake

So Bill you attempted to contact North Korea the other day via Bull horn...how did it go??
It was actually a nite time operation...
Café Gatto Nero
Cake

and it was actually carried out somewhat secretively...
Gatto

...that is if you like your job...your life... that sort of thing...
Cake

Ha yeah thats a good one Bill... so what actually happened...
Café Gatto Nero

Café Gatto Nero
Gatto
Cak
Well as you know the North Koreans can be a somewhat bellicose bunch..and when I was asked to try and get their attention with a bull horn I felt like I was a support act in a Charlie Chaplin skit..

arh.. Charlie Chaplin...one of the greats...it's small wonder many consider him with a kind of religious reverence...
Yes..you'd be hard pressed to beat him...slipping on an unseen banana skin has never been carried out with such....
Cake

Yes we're leaving the topic a little but did you hear about the Charlie Chaplin look alike competition he entered??
No...
I don't believe I did
Cake

He came third!
Café Gatto

Cake

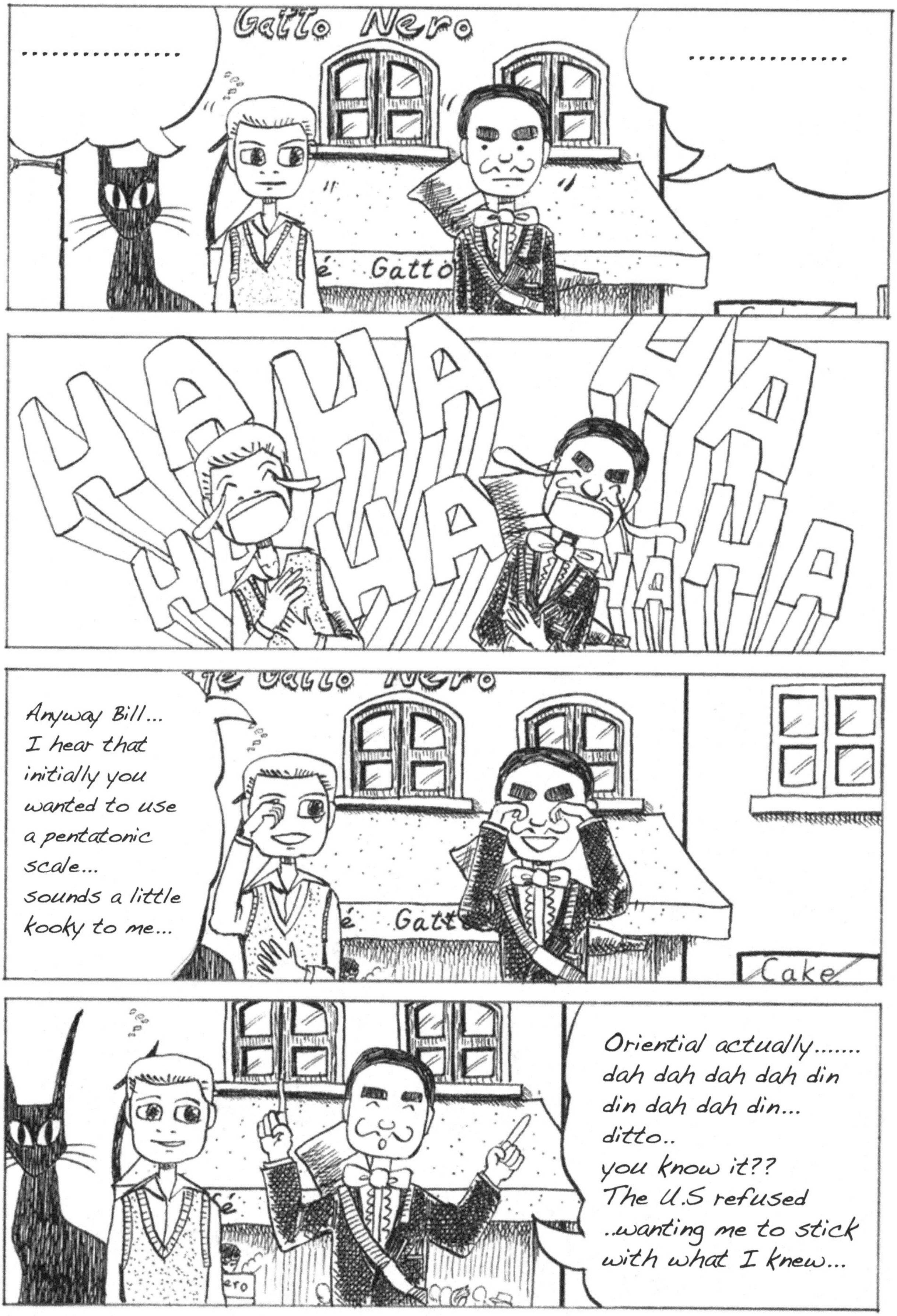

Gatto Nero

....

....

HAHAHAHAHAHAHAHA

Didnt you argue the Koreans would respond more favourably to a tune they knew??
Well it was made up in Japan that one...but I am sure they would recognize it...even if it did sound a little funny coming from a bull horn..

Café Gatto Nero
This guy doesn't need a bull horn to sound funny...
Caused quite a kerfuffle that one... tried to pitch the pentatonic idea by incorporating a few carefully choreographed dance steps...

Café Gatto Nero
..you dance also...
Cake

Yeah...
Fred Estaire...
singing in the rain..
that sort of thing...
Cake

Café Gatto Nero
Good... until I lost control and twirled into the nearest available ditch...
..wow... how did that come across...

Ouch!
Ouch alright....after that we had to go back to C major... they wouldn't come around to my way of thinking...looking like someone making it up I had nothing to fall back on...

I so want to stitch this interview up....
I guess you were pleased to finally get out of there...

Café
Nero
Nero
Yeah...only managed to get to f sharp before they started to fire at us...there was even some Korean announcement over the P.A system... really angry like..our interpreter informed us later it went something like' move now and forever hold that piece!...this was followed by' or you won't have long to live...get it!'...or words to that effect....we got out of there just in time...

Gatto Nero
..and was it worth the risk?
Yes...my mum always said: In this life you have to take the bull by the horns and I think she had a point...possibly two...

Café Gatto Nero
Thanks for your time Bill and good luck with that Bad horn
...opps I mean Bull horn of yours...
Thanks...
Café Gatto
Cake

This is Jack Binstalkin for Whirled News: Coming to a town named YOU!

Whirled
News

Café Gotto
Caf

Well as you can see we definitely have a situation up there... what do you make of it Barbie?

Well..it ain't wine and roses... didn't Martin Amis call the North Korean outfit an 'axis of evil?'
That doesn't surprise me...they've been blowing up a lot lately...to be Frank...not my real name..I think they were lucky to get out in one piece...

Quite...and speaking of pieces...I really liked the little ditty he knocked out..even if it did go a little ditto...

Oh...is that the time...looks like we've finally reached the end of another episode of 'Whirled News: Coming to a town named YOU!

Until next time it's good nite from me...and..
...arh it's still morning honey

And...have a good one people...

Do you want to have children?

Yes...that's where you come in...

GLUG
GLUG
GLUG
SNAP!
SMASH
what is this woman trying to do to me??..is she for real?
hello...Tinea here but I'm not....so please leave a message after my tone.. ticttt..sht...dooott!

hey Tinea its Bic
can you plea..-
..oh..hey Bic..
hows tricks?
well hey presto just
became O.M.G ....W.T.F
wha..what do you
mean?
you know damn well what I mean..what's the idea of bringing Bill Bender into it...this is not what I wrote and it certainly is not my idea of being funny...
well..I ..thought..
I don't pay you to think..and if the U.S military come looking for me I'm sending them your way...got it?
HENDRICK'S GIN
so why d'ya do it..huh?
talk to me
..uhh...I respect you as an artist Bic ...but as a respected artist in my own right I did it for my fans...

..fans..what fans?!
yeah...fans Bic...they have been with me since I don't know when..they..
..they blow me away!
ok...look I'm going turn a blind eye to this
but when I say verbatim...I mean it!!
ver..bat..umm?
yeah...you heard it right sugar...verbatim...its latin for 'word for word' ..got it?
yes ..but why are you talking like youre starring in a detective spoof written by Woody Allen.
...yeah they all wrote them...Thurber...Coren..I guess it's in my blood cupcake...
..and one more thing...the whole thing is too realistic...I want a more cartoon feel for the next one...can you do it?

..yes...I read you..
I'm not sure anyone else would!
thanks...over and not necessarily out...
ciao

A FEW SCENES LATER

The Melbourne bar review...
how it all went down...

that looks about as appetizing as a poorly presented petrie dish..way past petrified..

If only the elders would let me dive bomb for fish my way...chest first..yeah that's right baby..
Talk about the school of hard knocks-Ed
TAP
TAP

DJ CONNOR

love is a striking example of how little reality means to us...possibly attributed to Parcel Proust... I agree with that...

...ok lets wrap this up..
er...Bic...arh...hello...wrapping things up usually comes at the end..
er...sorry I guess it all started going wrong for me on waking up this morning... YOU try getting into a fresh pair of underwear the wrong way...

Ok... places please...
..er..Bic...dont we need to rehearse of something?

..what do you mean rehearse...those days are long gone...as in TRUMPERY... You think Davis and his crew rehearsed for Kind of Blue?
...yeah ...kind of...
well...they didn't...read the book..The Making of Kind of Blue...

Action I've got so much to give...I want to give it...I want to get some to..
Remember this will be on youtube later today...lets do it in one take
..I want a spontaneous improvisatory feel..
Goodmorning... afternnoon...evening or maybe youre in another time zone altogether...
Welcome to Melbourne one of the worlds hot spots for creativity...if you write, play music, write plays that could use some direction or just pretend to.. come on down...we'd love to hear from you! We are conveniently located somewhere off the west coast of New Zealand...
Anyway on with the show... Without being too mysterious about it we are reviewing all of the kool bars in Melbournes CBD..proving that Melbourne has a lot more on offer than just parking tickets...
Want to know more?

MELBOURNE BARS: THE HOT ONE HUNDRED... you coming?
TAP
TAP
TAP
KRUNCH!
you ok??
..yes..yes...at least the footage is realistic... so its not all in vein...
now where's Duncan?
hopefully not drunk
...oh Lord help us...
remembrance of things past is not necessarily remembrance of things as they were...and rest assured this guy aint going to remember anything...

I love you Sandy...
oh...
DJ CONNOR
Yeah baby tonight, the DJ got us fallin in love again

SMASH!

I'm going to call the police!! you ^&%*
...&%%*...&%*%&

arh...hel..lo...I will not be spoken to like that!

what fresh brouhaha is this??
I...I..'ave fame...ill...e ...issues ..that will never be fully dissolved..
HA HA HA
HA HA HA

this guys a little behind the eight ball.
...and thats our cue for an exit...
BAF
Whirled News!

Good morning and welcome to...
...er..its actually afternoon here Barbie...

Well so it is...anyway..as I was saying Good afternoon and welcome to another edition of 'Whirled News: Coming to a town named YOU!'
A cosmetic smile that is made up more than anything

Well did you get that Teddie... arh come in Teddie.. are you reading... or is it my turn??

...It's a little too early for S.N.A.F.U... and no that ain't a new board game...

Well ...did you get that Teddie
No

Excuse me?... what do you mean?
I mean... what if you don't live near any town... how could Whirled news possibly be...

I...well..I never thought of it like that...
..I wonder if the ear piece is interfering with his ability to operate his brain... that's the picture I'm getting...along with about Three million other viewers...

Have you heard the latest?
..no Barbie... I don't believe I have... what gives?

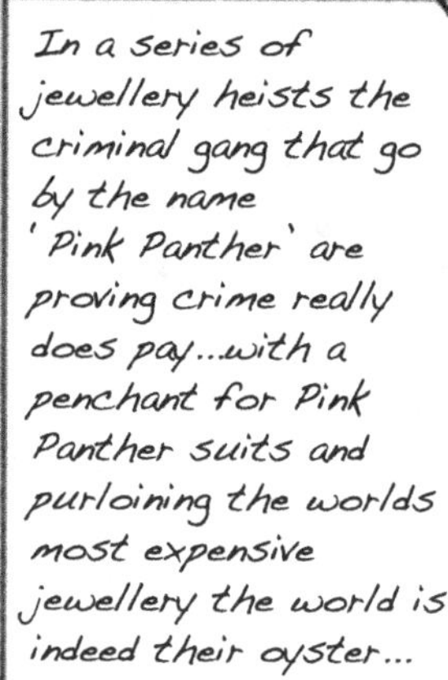
In a series of jewellery heists the criminal gang that go by the name 'Pink Panther' are proving crime really does pay...with a penchant for Pink Panther suits and purloining the worlds most expensive jewellery the world is indeed their oyster...

Yes..
I agree with you...
Well I'm actually paid to aren't I
Their most recent racket involved making out... opps I mean off with the world most expensive diamond necklace...

Unbelievable... does anyone happen to be on their case Teddie??
Thats a fine question Barbie and one in which I'm pleased you asked...

Well...
IS THERE??
This guy sure could use a little pick-me-up on the upper slopes...
This girls oblivious impetulance makes her sound like an out-patient that shouldn't be anywhere near out!
Yes Barbie..he goes by the name Inspector Cluedo...

What?!
..not the famous Italian investigator in ..
No...he is Italian though and he is famous..he invented the board game cluedo... if he cant catch these guys nobody can...

We going for an all exclusive interview with Jack Binstalkin to possibly hear all about it?
It's all part of the show Barbie..let's go live now to our reporter Jack Binstalkin and find out whether Cluedo is any closer to catching these crazy cats...
Put it this way... Jack in the beanstalk..
Er its Binstalkin sir...

Well whatever it is... put it this way... amongst the criminal fraternity these guys certainly are a sell out!...apart from looking like the cartoon character that goes by the same name in every other respect these guys are thoughly professional...

Sorry to interrupt sir but what'll it be?
Just three double shot expressos on the double...

Coffee good?

My word...
its a caffine hit
that feels like youve
been hit over the
head by a ...
!!
!!

Arhh...
I don't mean
literally fool!!
sorry
sorry
Fascinating Clueso
you mean to...
Tap..
Tap..!!
Tap..!
Its Cluedo
..like the board
game...FOOL!
Oh yeah...
so you're saying
these guys mimic
crimes found
in the Peter
Sellers
movie?

I didn't actually say that... but you're right that's exactly what they do..we've caught most of their crimes on CCTV and invariably we have Pink Suited Panthers moving amongst the shadows... AND THAT BLASTED THEME MUSIC!!!..
They're obviously having a field day..
They are... although admittedly most of it is at night... It's a game of cat and mouse that frankly I wished I had never got caught up in...
You were saying earlier they have a dance routine as well..
Yes...it's carefully choreographed to match the theme music perfectly...
You mean... do..do.....do..do.. do..do..

ARGGGH... stop it... I can't take it anymore....
Hmm...I guess anyone would be happy lifting the worlds most expensive diamond...
Yes..it's something to marvel at... ...or at least it was...
Cheer up old chap... I hope you have better luck next time in catching a little more than the tail end of their exit...
This is Jack Binstalkin for another world exclusive on Whirled news: coming to a town named YOU!
What do you make of it Barbie...looks like Cluedo has his hands full..

Yes well they certainly have...interestingly enough Teddie there has now been a stage adaptation of how these guys came about...their inception if you will... before they became successful enough to fly between crime scenes...
Fascinating Barbie... where's it set??

A dilapidated blancmange factory on the outskirts of Bulgeria...
Sure sounds like a mouthful...

In case you've just joined us I'm Barbie Brouhaha and this is Whirled News ..What's hot Teddie?
Well this is Whirled News.. want to be spun out?

try me...
Well I hear they rated Peter Cook as the funniest comedian of all time...but hey thats understandable..and North Koreas latest exploits in the arena of nuclear testing have been a blast with everything going to pieces shortly after takeoff...gave everyone a hell of a fright...

Yes... the North Koreans certainly have become a reliable source of breaking news and it's hard to keep up at times

And now for the news.. It turns out the pressure really is on for kindy kids these days.. Good hand shake...firm eye contact...a knowledge of ballroom etiquette ..these are all highly sought after attributes any successful five year old should have if he wants to get into an elementary school affiliated with the Ivy League ..

11

wowsa... these kids start early huh?
Yes it's the way of the world Barbie...for years it was merely preparing for standardized I.Q tests intended to break all but the top 2%...but it appears they've taken this stultiloquence to the next level..
Stultiloquence... sounds like you're leaving me behind..
Mumbo jumbo... my dear..
So how do the kids prepare for the testing Teddie?
Thats a very good question Barbie... and one which I'm pleased you asked...they formed a company called Ciceros Circle..
Fascinating Teddy... whos Cicero...
I wish they would give me the script occasionally... it's embarrassing
Oh just some famous Psychiatrist circa 200 BC...

What the??!
...He was actually a philosopher... they didn't actually have Psychiatry back then..
Well thats news to me Teddie...have we got an interview to go on...
That's what we are here for... Barbie..we caught up with the founder of Ciceros Circle...or at least Jack Binstalkin did..lets go take a look..
Hello and welcome to another edition of Whirled News: Coming to a town near you...

I'm Jack and the Beanstalk...
opps I mean Jack Binstalkin.. and with us in the studio today we have Simone Simons
Hi Beanstalk...
opps I mean Binstalkin... welcome
Er...Jacks just fine Si-money...
Its pronounced 'sigh-moan' and if you get it wrong again I'm out of here...
So prep school to prepare school kids for yale huh...How do you do it?...and more to the point why do you do it??!..dont you think the kids of today have enough pressure to deal with...
Oh...nonsense Jack...if it wasn't for the inception of our Mock Play Date® half these kids wouldn't make it..

So what do you actually do to them?

Er..rather..
I mean what do you actually do for these kids?
We take them through a battery of tests, with our raft of educational consultants observing..

And what do you actually test?
Oh just everything...from tying a Windsor without going suicidal.. conversational French...and counting out the correct change at a Mcdonalds drive in..it's all there...

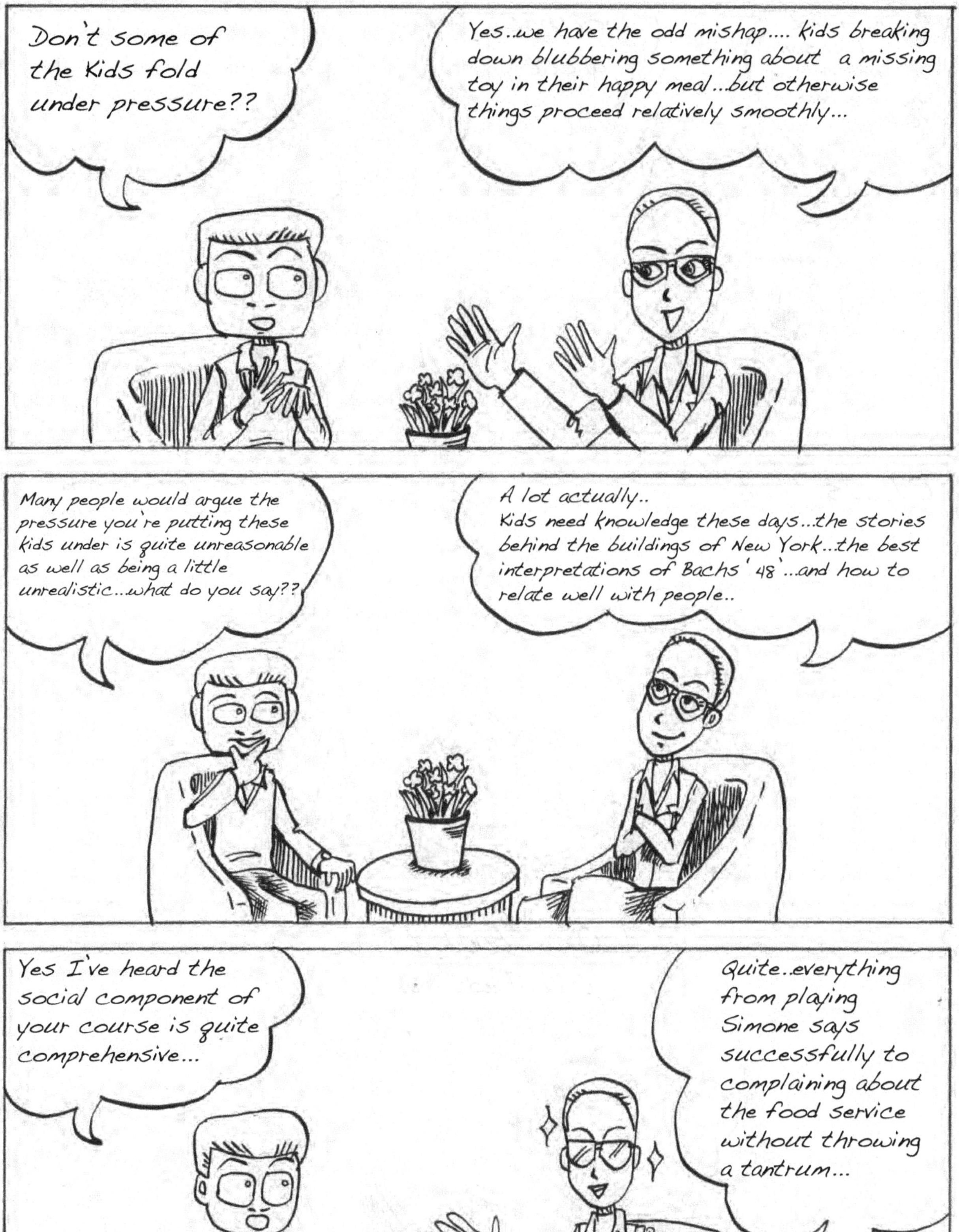

Don't some of the Kids fold under pressure??

Yes..we have the odd mishap.... kids breaking down blubbering something about a missing toy in their happy meal...but otherwise things proceed relatively smoothly...

Many people would argue the pressure you're putting these kids under is quite unreasonable as well as being a little unrealistic...what do you say??

A lot actually..
Kids need knowledge these days...the stories behind the buildings of New York...the best interpretations of Bachs' 48'...and how to relate well with people..

Remind me not to send my son or daughter anywhere near YOU!
Sounds great

Oh...is that the time
Yes you can find it on most watches...

Ok ...back to you Teddy...

So you have been through it Johannes Chrysostomus Theophilus...what was it like? ...by the way can I call you Theo?
Call me whatever you like ted...and a short introduction would of been nice...

Ciceros circus..opps I mean circle huh...your 450 page report here indicates you passed with flying colours...

zzz

Yes.. the conversational French was a cinch
I've been fluent in seventeen languages for as long as I can remember so this wasn't surprising...but identifying the different flags ships use as distress signals I ran into a few problems..

But you got most of them right...right??
Of course ..except the one that states "I need a tug"

Sounds a little off course to me..

And we understand Theo there is a short test to assess your suitability for Cireros Circle..

Yes on arrival we are instructed to mingle like one would at a cocktail party I guess...A team of psychologists disguised as window cleaners take notes as best they can... whilst some of the kids are quietly removed..

Fascinating...I guess parents are happy to exaggerate their childs achievement and some kids need all the help they can get...
I don't follow...what do you mean?

I mean..

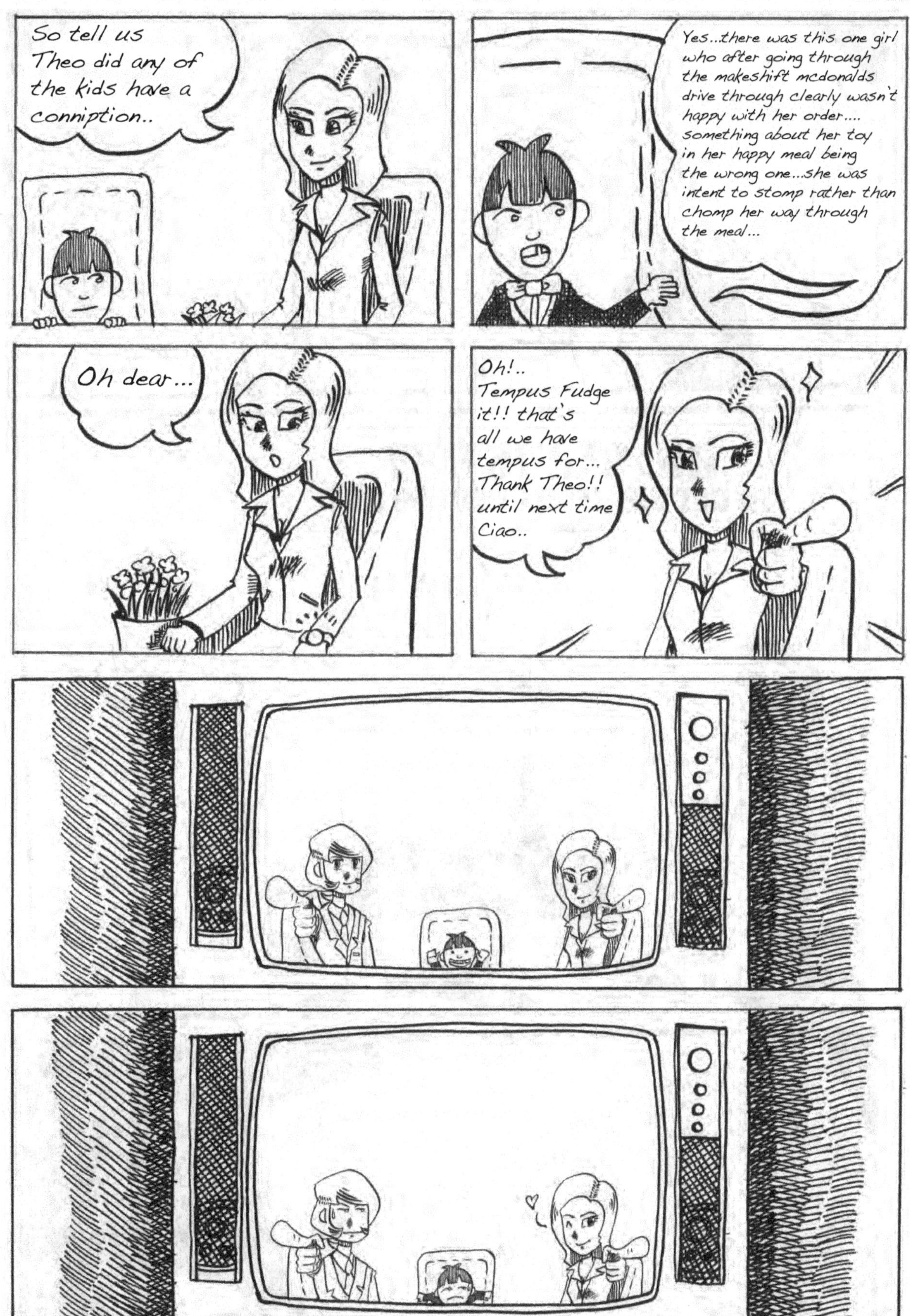
So tell us Theo did any of the kids have a conniption..
Yes..there was this one girl who after going through the makeshift mcdonalds drive through clearly wasn't happy with her order.... something about her toy in her happy meal being the wrong one...she was intent to stomp rather than chomp her way through the meal...
Oh dear...
Oh!.. Tempus Fudge it!! that's all we have tempus for... Thank Theo!! until next time Ciao..

wha...appen..d?.....
?

BIC HEADS OUT
TO GET HIS HEAD CHECKED OUT
you... you look drawn out! ...how would you describe your sleep Bic?
er... ...possibly a series of mismanaged microsleeps..

Patients having issues sleeping. His expression wouldn't be out of place in an infomercial that addresses the suffering surrounding sleep deprivation. You know: Partially asymmetrical mouth, saliva hanging precariously, and the odd piece of theatrical thrashing around punching at the air for effect.
hmm...I see...

yes...microsleeping is frustrating all round.. the sheep?...even their attempt at the bar is cut short...
how's school?
sigh ..you don't want to know...
go on..

...I can't go on..the general malaise is insipid...a spreading atrophy of sorts that aimlessly wanders from vacuous vapidity to graffiti that reads: 'SUCKS SHIT FROM ASS!'
..hmm...anyway moving right along... we need to run you through a few tests Bic..

...what sort of tests??

well initially just a general I.Q test ...if that's alright with you..
sounds fun...
I'm just going to make some notes...

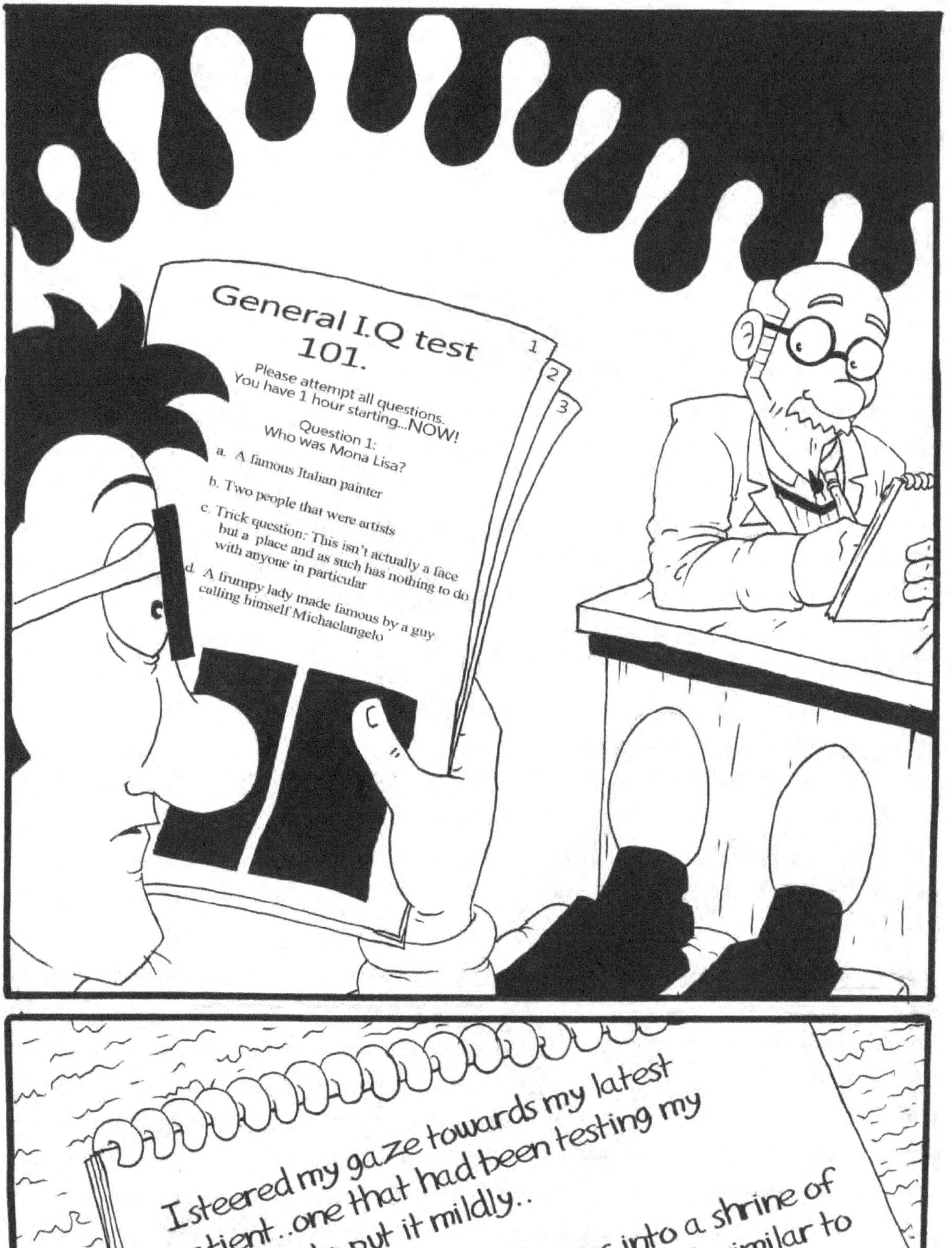

General I.Q test 101.

Please attempt all questions.
You have 1 hour starting...NOW!

Question 1:
Who was Mona Lisa?

a. A famous Italian painter

b. Two people that were artists

c. Trick question: This isn't actually a face but a place and as such has nothing to do with anyone in particular

d. A frumpy lady made famous by a guy calling himself Michaelangelo

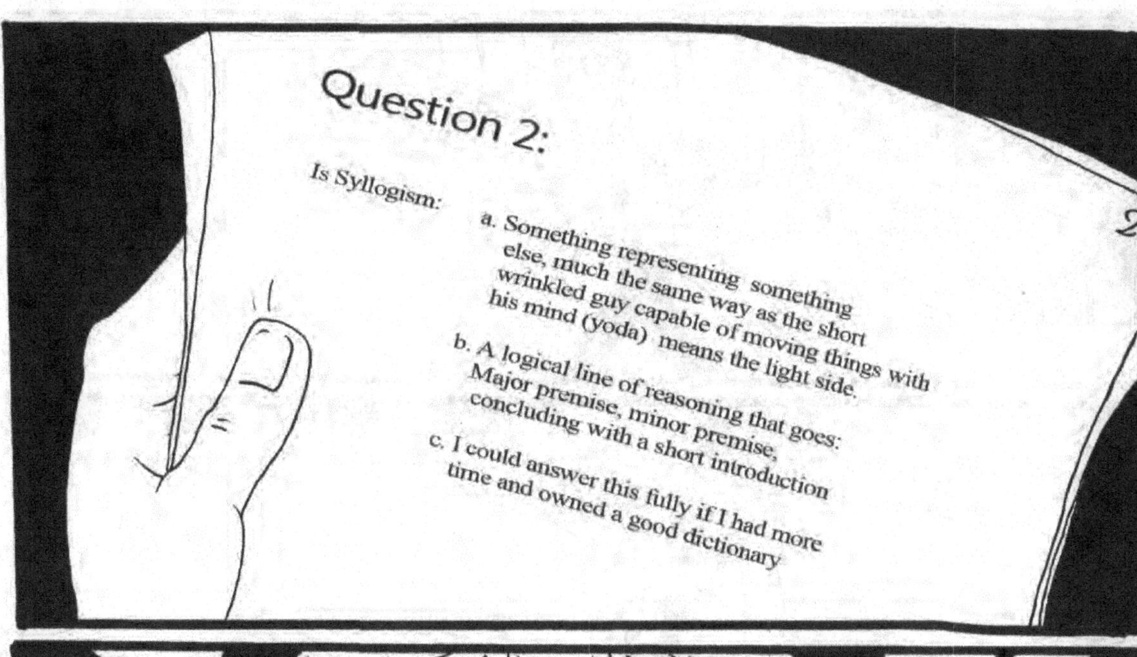
Question 2:
Is Syllogism:
a. Something representing something else, much the same way as the short wrinkled guy capable of moving things with his mind (yoda) means the light side.
b. A logical line of reasoning that goes: Major premise, minor premise, concluding with a short introduction
c. I could answer this fully if I had more time and owned a good dictionary
2

3
Question 3:
In Prousts "In search of Lost Time" what was he getting at?
a. He set out to prove irrefutably that by using sentences a little short of one km in length it is possible to write a novel of such unfathomable length that time no longer means anything
b. You can't actually find lost time and its a good idea to get your watch regularly serviced
c. Being bedridden for fourteen years gives one a lot of time to think

DR. FU MANCHU
(OXFORD)
M.A.D.D.AS
(YALE)
P.O.C.O.L.O.C.O
(HARDLY)
thanks Dr Fu.. certainly gave me a lot to chew on..catch you on the blip side...

THERAPIST
DR. FU MANCHU
M.A.D.D.AS
(YALE)
O.C.O.L.O.C.O

SOME EIGHTEEN MONTHS EARLIER...
...so yeah dad I'm going to do it...I'm going to Korea to teach English for a year..
LATIN-KOREAN DICTIONARY
Korean Dictionary
LETS SPEAK KOREAN!
KOREA

..you sure it's a sound career move?
..of course...I may even meet someone
sounds promising
Lord help us...
I've even started learning the language...
..challenging I bet...
yes..bought a Korean dictionary ..just going to throw together a few of my own phrases that I'll know I will need shortly after touch down...
I mean I don't want to appear like a complete nincompoop...
yeah... like 'have you got a light'.. heheh
Well before you skip the country, remember I am your landlord. AND. YOU. DO. OWE. ME. RENT... ..is that emphatic enough for you...
..yes ..you'll get your money pops... gotta bounce...call you when I'm about to board the plane..
ok ciao..
ciao

Nomu..piss..a yo..
(I SEEM TO BE..)
chom...gakka...juseyo-yo?
(..A LITTLE SHORT..CAN YOU COVER THIS?)
LET'S SPEAK KOREAN
Nomu pissayo chom gakka juseyo-yo?
(I SEEM TO BE A LITTLE SHORT, CAN YOU COVER THIS?)
Igol...mwo..rago..
(ARE ALL THE TOILETS..)
LET'S SPEAK KOREAN!
..pulleyo-yo?!
(..AND WHAT DO YOU CALL THAT?!)
Igol mworago pulley-yo?!
(ARE ALL THE TOILETS FLUSH WITH THE FLOOR AND WHAT DO YOU CALL THAT?!)
Er...Chal...doe..gil..
(HOW MUCH IS YOUR..)
..pir..oyo Konbae?
(..CHEAPEST WHISKEY?)
LET'S SPEAK KOREA
Er...Chal doegil piroyo Konbae?
(ER..HOW MUCH IS YOUR CHEAPEST WHISKEY?)

Chega chew..
(YOU FROM...)
LET'S SPEAK KOREAN!

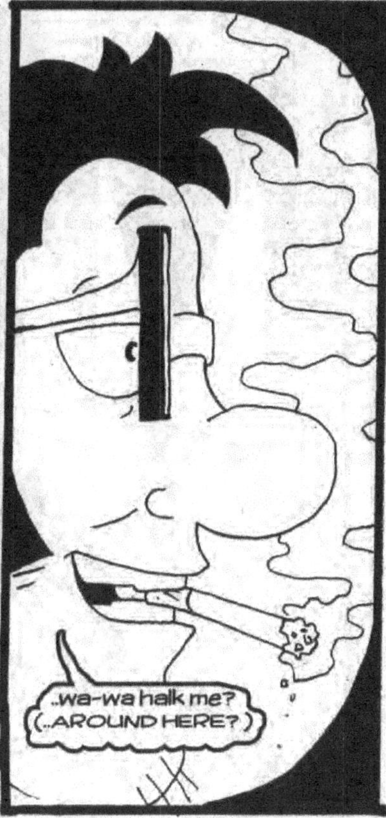
..wa-wa halk me?
(..AROUND HERE?)

Chega chew wa-wa halk me?
(YOU FROM AROUND HERE?)
LET'S SPEAK KOREAN!

Chibe kayagess..
oyo hae..yo...
(IT'S RATHER NOISY IN HERE...)
..haeya issoyo sangwa?
(..WANT TO GO OUTSIDE AND LOOK FOR SOME FRESH AIR?)
Chibe kayagessoyo
haeyo issoyo sangwa?
(IT'S RATHER NOISY IN HERE... WANT TO GO OUTSIDE AND LOOK FOR SOME FRESH AIR?)

Sarang..ahae
to-you....
(WE COULD ALWAYS HIT MY..)
...aparto Ondol..
(..APARTMENT AND CHECK OUT THE UNDERFLOOR HEATING)
Sarangahae
to-you apar
to ondol
(WE COULD ALWAYS HIT MY APARTMENT AND CHECK OUT THE UNDERFLOOR HEATING..)
LET'S SPEAK KOREAN!

Punny jusiknow On-doll...doll! (FUNNY HOW IT'S CALLED ON-DOLL...DOLL!)

Ow...corsaw! (OW...THAT HURT!)

Aju kup bok-boo, pisang satea rushee...to...ar...er...EYO!! (WHERE IS THE NEAREST TOILET, AND I'M NOT TALKING ABOUT THE KIMCHI SQUAT...QUICKLY PLEASE ...IT'S...AR...ER...URGENT!!)

Haek shilhom... igot chayon pohoo Kuyogieyo? (WHAT'S UP WITH THE GUY UP NORTH...IS HE OUT TO LAUNCH?)

Towajuseyo
(I DONT FEEL SAFE)
LETS SPEAK KOREAN!

LET'S SPEAK KOREA
Ju ding-dong too... saengniga opsoyo? (WHEN ARE WE GOING HOME?)

Dong wong opps up??
(WHERE AM I??)

Juseyo mumsy!
(I WANT MUMSY!)

Ijiyoge, pukan kanch odi issulsudo issoyo?..
(YEAH, WHATS YOUR CHEAPEST FLIGHT OUT OF HERE??..)
..chimyongdongwong!.. innun sanghwangchang!!
(...I DON'T CARE!..ANYWHERE WILL DO!!)

Tilley TrilBy's
Catch You on the Blip Side...

TEACHING

Thinking of joining the teaching profession? Well with what little mind you've left that's still operational, think again.

All schools are as incomprehensible as they are unintelligible and good luck in trying to decipher any of it.

What follows is an extensive but by no means exhaustive inventory of the inherent demands and in some case dangers of the teaching profession.

A discourse if you like of those potential hazards that threaten to put you off-course the moment you step into the place.

As a teacher there is little need to spell out that you are fully immersed in a milieu governed by its own laws and systems that by and large, are particularly efficacious at turning you into a basket case (usually by degrees.)

These difficulties, at once unavoidable as they are insurmountable confront you on a daily basis as an in-your-face feature of just being there. And yes, just like the cataclysmic trajectory of a prize fighters final blow the whole thing has an unstoppable certainty best described as impatient.

A is for A4. It's paper. Its prolific promulgation has implications, like being overwhelmed in a particularly unmanageable way.

Whether it's the paper plane variety thrown around by the class clown convinced that this remains the ne plus ultra of light entertainment or something a little more official, memorandums, reports, that sort of thing, its just everywhere. It's exuberant abundance is plenarious, covering everything, including you!

Filing cabinets, cupboards, draws, desks; they are all cluttered with the stuff, like it really does grow on trees.

It lends itself well to a certain casus belli or in plain English a war on paper.

It insidiously swamps you; stack upon stack of the stuff takes center stage at your desk and this disorganized disarray remains a permanent fixture shortly after you say, 'just leave it on my desk will you'. It's dangerous. Forget paper cuts, it's psychological.
It's just a sign of the times: volume of paper = accurate assessment on productivity.

Finding a place for it all isaproblem of daunting dimensions and I suggest you just let it go.

The Romans quite rightly referred to it as a pons asinorum. Just remember to breathe and under NO CIRCUMSTANCES try to physically fight the stuff, you'll only end up hurting yourself.

Concerning what ends up on your desk much of it can safely be ignored, like the illegible scrawls for teachers detailing what to do next. In fact don't think twice about biffing any of it.

IF the principal approaches you about the seven page report on Mr Misdemeanour that was required yesterday feign innocence. Possibly a little fried upstairs , don't let your exaggerated gesticulations get out of hand and keep phrases like ' LOOK, I DIDN"T DO IT OK!' to a minimum.
Make a memorandum to yourself to turn over a new leaf and commence every Monday morning with quietly disposing of your desk top. No exceptions.

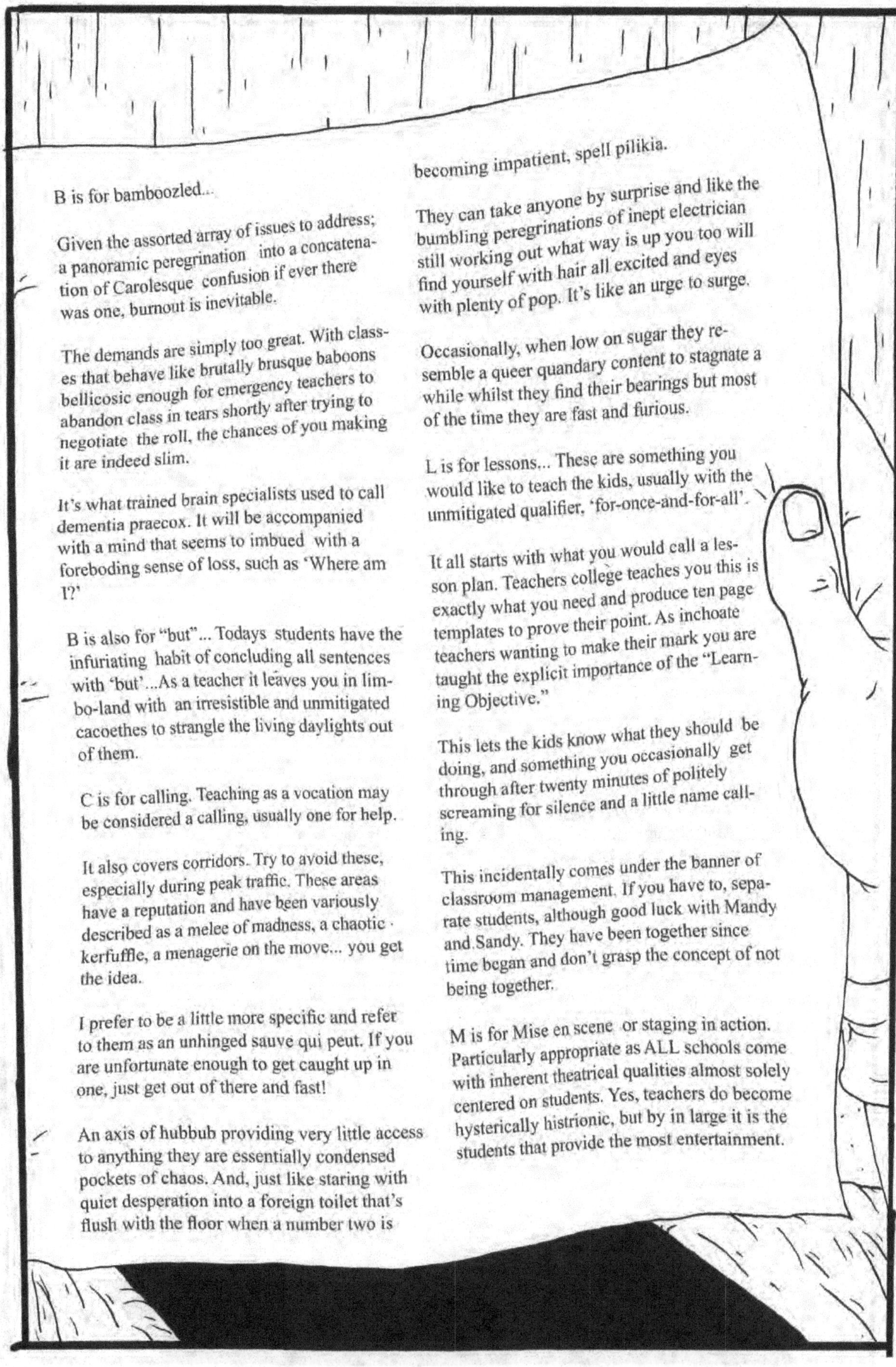

B is for bamboozled...

Given the assorted array of issues to address; a panoramic peregrination into a concatenation of Carolesque confusion if ever there was one, burnout is inevitable.

The demands are simply too great. With classes that behave like brutally brusque baboons bellicosic enough for emergency teachers to abandon class in tears shortly after trying to negotiate the roll, the chances of you making it are indeed slim.

It's what trained brain specialists used to call dementia praecox. It will be accompanied with a mind that seems to imbued with a foreboding sense of loss, such as 'Where am I?'

B is also for "but"... Todays students have the infuriating habit of concluding all sentences with 'but'...As a teacher it leaves you in limbo-land with an irresistible and unmitigated cacoethes to strangle the living daylights out of them.

C is for calling. Teaching as a vocation may be considered a calling, usually one for help.

It also covers corridors. Try to avoid these, especially during peak traffic. These areas have a reputation and have been variously described as a melee of madness, a chaotic kerfuffle, a menagerie on the move... you get the idea.

I prefer to be a little more specific and refer to them as an unhinged sauve qui peut. If you are unfortunate enough to get caught up in one, just get out of there and fast!

An axis of hubbub providing very little access to anything they are essentially condensed pockets of chaos. And, just like staring with quiet desperation into a foreign toilet that's flush with the floor when a number two is becoming impatient, spell pilikia.

They can take anyone by surprise and like the bumbling peregrinations of inept electrician still working out what way is up you too will find yourself with hair all excited and eyes with plenty of pop. It's like an urge to surge.

Occasionally, when low on sugar they resemble a queer quandary content to stagnate a while whilst they find their bearings but most of the time they are fast and furious.

L is for lessons... These are something you would like to teach the kids, usually with the unmitigated qualifier, 'for-once-and-for-all'.

It all starts with what you would call a lesson plan. Teachers college teaches you this is exactly what you need and produce ten page templates to prove their point. As inchoate teachers wanting to make their mark you are taught the explicit importance of the "Learning Objective."

This lets the kids know what they should be doing, and something you occasionally get through after twenty minutes of politely screaming for silence and a little name calling.

This incidentally comes under the banner of classroom management. If you have to, separate students, although good luck with Mandy and Sandy. They have been together since time began and don't grasp the concept of not being together.

M is for Mise en scene or staging in action. Particularly appropriate as ALL schools come with inherent theatrical qualities almost solely centered on students. Yes, teachers do become hysterically histrionic, but by in large it is the students that provide the most entertainment.

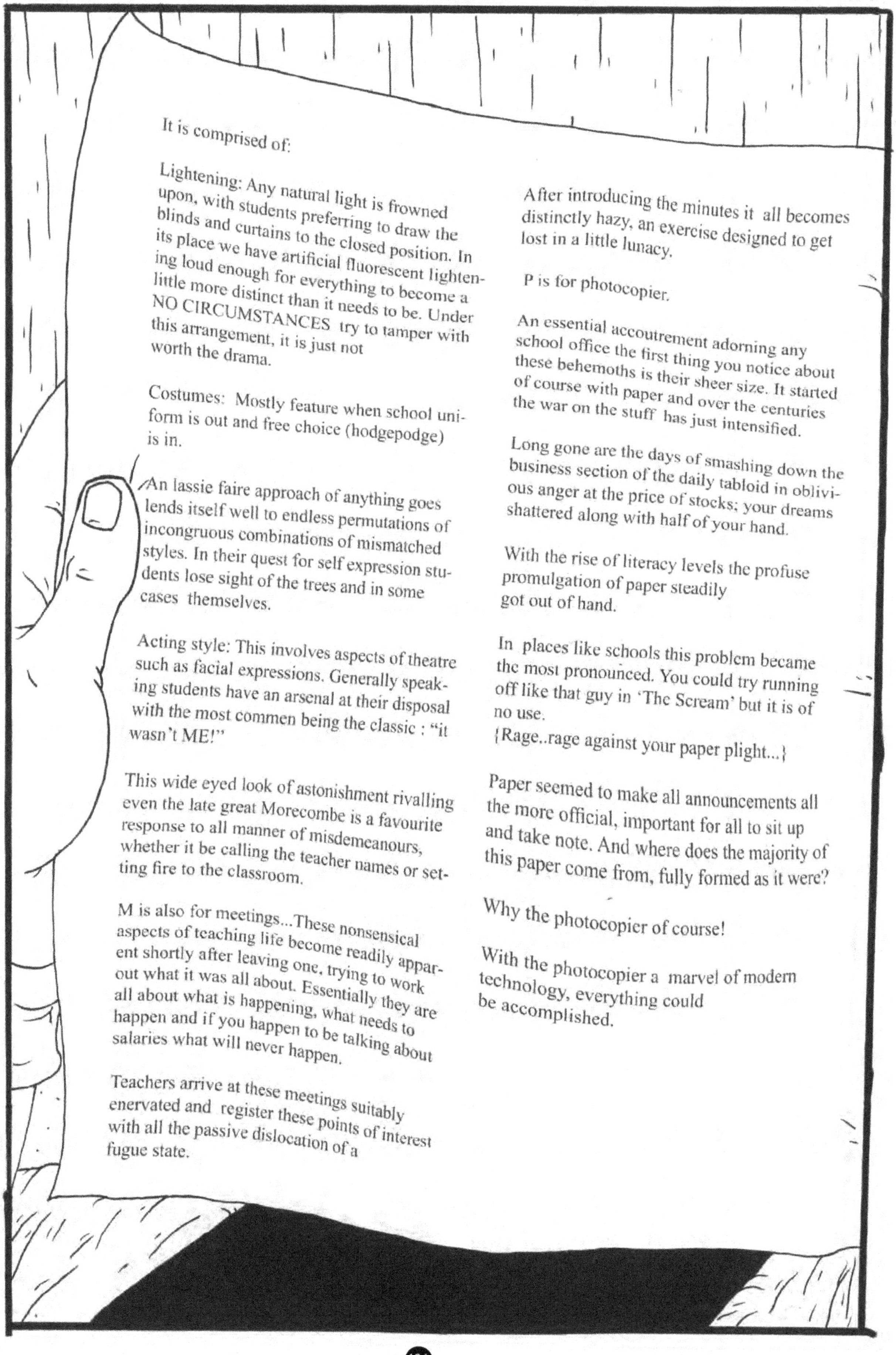

It is comprised of:

Lightening: Any natural light is frowned upon, with students preferring to draw the blinds and curtains to the closed position. In its place we have artificial fluorescent lightening loud enough for everything to become a little more distinct than it needs to be. Under NO CIRCUMSTANCES try to tamper with this arrangement, it is just not worth the drama.

Costumes: Mostly feature when school uniform is out and free choice (hodgepodge) is in.

An lassie faire approach of anything goes lends itself well to endless permutations of incongruous combinations of mismatched styles. In their quest for self expression students lose sight of the trees and in some cases themselves.

Acting style: This involves aspects of theatre such as facial expressions. Generally speaking students have an arsenal at their disposal with the most commen being the classic : "it wasn't ME!"

This wide eyed look of astonishment rivalling even the late great Morecombe is a favourite response to all manner of misdemeanours, whether it be calling the teacher names or setting fire to the classroom.

M is also for meetings...These nonsensical aspects of teaching life become readily apparent shortly after leaving one, trying to work out what it was all about. Essentially they are all about what is happening, what needs to happen and if you happen to be talking about salaries what will never happen.

Teachers arrive at these meetings suitably enervated and register these points of interest with all the passive dislocation of a fugue state.

After introducing the minutes it all becomes distinctly hazy, an exercise designed to get lost in a little lunacy.

P is for photocopier.

An essential accoutrement adorning any school office the first thing you notice about these behemoths is their sheer size. It started of course with paper and over the centuries the war on the stuff has just intensified.

Long gone are the days of smashing down the business section of the daily tabloid in oblivious anger at the price of stocks; your dreams shattered along with half of your hand.

With the rise of literacy levels the profuse promulgation of paper steadily got out of hand.

In places like schools this problem became the most pronounced. You could try running off like that guy in 'The Scream' but it is of no use.
{Rage..rage against your paper plight...}

Paper seemed to make all announcements all the more official, important for all to sit up and take note. And where does the majority of this paper come from, fully formed as it were?

Why the photocopier of course!

With the photocopier a marvel of modern technology, everything could be accomplished.

Class sets, school sets. Double sided sets, collation, triple sided sets, folded, stapled, memorandums on memorandums, reports passing comment on why people didn't pass, wireless at a speed suggesting teachers haven't got time to wait.

Impressive as they are with their sheer size and intricate key pad design, whose possible permutations look to be approaching the infinite, you would think they would make teachers lives easier. On the contrary.

They invariably fail teachers in the minute of their greatest need, that being the one immediately after their class was due to commence.

They are, without putting too finer point on it, a frenzied flurry of frazzle; being conductive to leaving the national guidelines of where blood pressure should be altogether.

The problem falls into two well defined categories.

There is category one: Failing to follow teacher instruction, or 'What the #@*%!'

Despite carefully keying in instructions at a speed suggesting things are a little slow on the upper slopes pages come at you that are all as blank as your stare.

In a maelstrom of something certifiable, you can frantically stab at the clear button all you want, nothing will alter the copiers current course. A whirlwind of warm and unusually white paper will continue to be spat at you with enough eager-to-please enthusiasm to be down-right diversivolent.

This will continue until however long it takes. Everyone has a breaking point and eventually your flaming fantods, driven to distraction, will begin looking further afield to assess the frangibility of nearby objects.
Like the glass-screen.

It's just plain stupid.

Teachers in the queue behind start fidgeting nervously before sidling off sympathetically. They simply don't want to be caught up in it all, and who could blame them.

Category two involves the paper jam, or "This is not happening!" It's an exercise in fault finding. With approximately too many trays that fold out, pull out, push out or are simply ornamental,being confounded comes with the territory. Usually a paper jam begins with a characteristically grinding halt to something that, prior to this sounded very busy. The uncomfortable silence is accompanied by a flashing control panel emphatically stating something about a CODE 51. Occasionally they will throw in a tray number. To avoid disappointment take this with a grain of salt, remembering to breathe as you valiantly announce to the teacher behind you you are going in. Or maybe you can just leave...

R is for report writing...This dreaded exercise in futility usually follows a semesters teaching or at least trying it. Moving through the various stages of production it comes with its own inherent challenges best described as extreme.

The problems usually commence with teachers getting down to actually starting them. It is an arduous task that very few teachers enjoy and as such the general approach is one of listless lethargy. At this point Senior management usually step in with words of encouragement, instilling into the tireless troops a sense of esprit de corp. That is until it dawns on them that with one week to go very few teachers are beyond 'B' and they may have to kill someone.

Proof reading reports in itself deserves a separate entry. It doesn't help that the people proofreading your reports happen to be experts in the English language.

Your reports come back to you immediately, ruined with red pen, wild annotations where they are needed. Something about being unable to have a past particulate anywhere near a conjunctive, particularly when you don't even know what tense you are writing in! {Lord make me an instrument of thy peace. Where there is hatred, love...ad infinitum}

Don't be surprised if the clique 'can do better' makes an appearance.

T is for...To whom it may concern, you are a concern! Or in plain English: a letter to yourself stating the obvious. It's a legitimate response to a fully blown burn out finally fizzing. Don't say I didn't warn you.

Y is for yard duty or 'Why me?'

Approach this thankless task with the stealth like caution it deserves. Without walls, a whiteboard and teacher taking centre stage, outside is so decidedly different. Best described as a type of purgatory for your past sins in this life and any other life you had before teaching. With a variety of settings to rival Dantes Inferno you simply must keep your wits about you.

Your patience will be tested and as a general rule, there are no rules. If at all possible they will take you by surprise.

Like dousing your leg in enough correction fluid to get it right the first time.

It's all about controlling your emotion but if you have to, go out with a bang.

This entails some adlibbed theatrics, such as a meek yet manically made up mumble, something along the lines of, "oh beseech me!" You can offset its obvious incoherence by convincing histrionics and role play, involving dead and rolling off towards stage left...

LETS SPEAK KOREAN!
THE END
(for now)